Th

Th
a

HiPPO OWNS UP

Written by Sue Graves

Illustrated by

Trevor Dunton

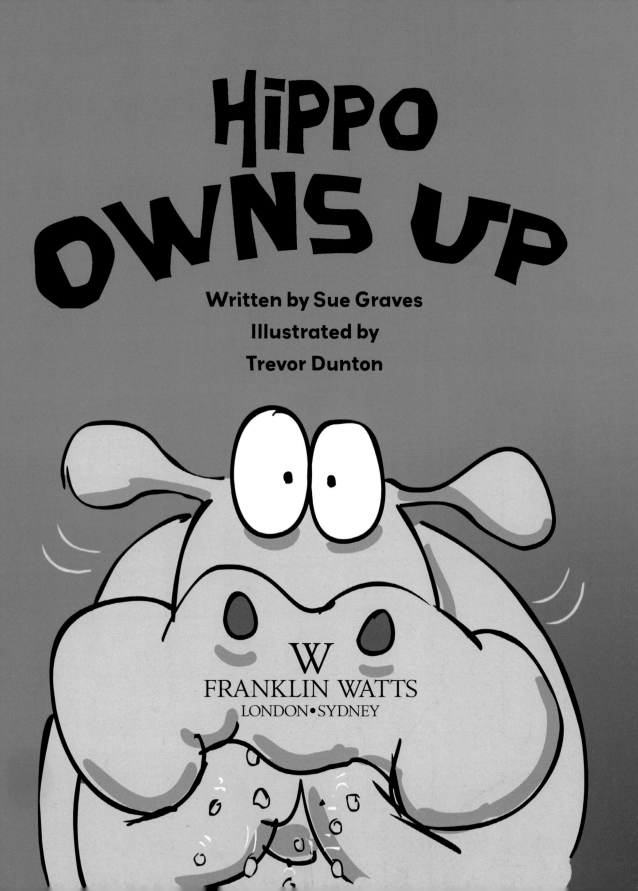

W

FRANKLIN WATTS

LONDON • SYDNEY

It was Tuesday and Hippo was having a **bad day**. He had got up late.

He had **missed breakfast**.

He was **late** for school, too.
Miss Bird was cross.

4

Then Miss Bird gave him lots of sums to do.
But Hippo was **too hungry** to do them.

Hippo looked at the clock. It was nearly lunchtime. Mrs Croc always made chocolate cake for lunch on Tuesdays. She always put lots of chocolate icing on the top, too.

RUMB

Hippo thought about the chocolate cake and the chocolate icing. His tummy **rumbled loudly**. Everyone heard. Everyone giggled.
Miss Bird told them to **get on with their work**.

But the more Hippo thought about the
chocolate cake, the louder his tummy
rumbled. Then he got the **hiccups**!
The hiccups were very, very loud.

Everyone laughed. Miss Bird got cross. She said Hippo was **disturbing everyone**. She told him to go to the kitchen to get a drink of water.

Hippo went to the kitchen. The big chocolate cake was on the table. He went to get a closer look. It looked **delicious**. It smelled **delicious**. He decided to try a tiny bit of it. He picked up a spoon and took a bit of cake.
It tasted wonderful!

Hippo stared at the cake. Now there was a little hole on one side of the cake. He tried to smooth the icing over the hole. But it looked worse. He took some cake from the other side to try to even it up. But it looked **worse** than before.

Hippo was **worried**. He wanted to make the cake look better. He took more and more cake. It tasted delicious, but the more he took, the worse it looked. Soon there was **no cake** left at all!

Hippo went back to class. Miss Bird said he had been a **long time**. She told him to **get on** with his sums.

But Hippo could not get on with his sums.

His tummy felt too full and he felt too sick.

He **felt bad** for eating all the cake.

Just then the bell rang for lunchtime. Everyone lined up. But Mrs Croc had some bad news. She said there was no chocolate cake because it had **all gone**. She said Hattie, the school cat, must have eaten it. She said Hattie was a bad cat. Hippo said **nothing**.

Everyone ate their lunch, but Hippo was **not hungry**. He was not hungry at all. Mrs Croc was worried.

Hippo was **always** hungry and he always ate his lunch. She thought he must be ill. She sent him to Miss Bird.

Hippo told Miss Bird about the chocolate cake. He told her that he had eaten it, not Hattie. Miss Bird said that he should **not** have eaten the cake but that he was brave **to own up**. She said he should have a good think about how to **put things right**.

Hippo had a good think. He told Miss Bird he had to **say sorry** to everyone for eating the cake. He said he had a **good idea** to put things right, too. He told Miss Bird his good idea. She said it was a very good one.

Hippo said **sorry** to everyone.

He said **sorry** to Mrs Croc.

He said **sorry** to Hattie the cat, too!

Then Hippo asked Mrs Croc if she would help him to bake a new chocolate cake for everyone. Mrs Croc gave him **lots of help**. Hippo baked a very good cake. It had lots of chocolate icing on the top, too.

Soon the cake was ready to eat. Everyone went to get a closer look. It looked **delicious**. It smelled **delicious**. Everyone took a bit of cake. It tasted **wonderful**! Hippo was pleased.

Hippo said he was glad he had **owned up** and **put things right**. Then Mrs Croc asked him if he would like some cake.

Hippo said he did not want any. He said he did not want any chocolate cake **ever again**! Everyone laughed.

A note about sharing this book

The *Behaviour Matters* series has been developed
to provide a starting point for further discussion on
children's behaviour both in relation to themselves
and others. The series is set in the jungle with
animal characters reflecting typical behaviour
traits often seen in young children.

Hippo Owns Up
This story explores the problems that arise when we do something
wrong, but then do not own up to it. It looks at the consequences of
our actions on others. The book also aims to encourage the children
to develop strategies in controlling their behaviour and examines ways
to put things right when they do something wrong.

How to use the book
The book is designed for adults to share with either an individual child,
or a group of children, and as a starting point for discussion.

The book also provides visual support and repeated words and phrases
to build reading confidence.

Before reading the story
Choose a time to read when you and the children are relaxed and have
time to share the story.

Spend time looking at the illustrations and talk about what the book
might be about before reading it together.

Encourage children to employ a phonics first approach to tackling
new words by sounding the words out.

After reading, talk about the book with the children:

- Talk about the story with the children. Encourage them to retell the events in chronological order.

- Ask them to express their opinions about Hippo's behaviour. Do they think he was wrong to let Hattie, the cat, take the blame? Should he have owned up sooner?

- Invite the children to relate their own experiences of owning up about something they have done wrong in the past to the others. How did they feel before they owned up? How did they feel afterwards? What consequences did their actions have on other people? Did someone else get blamed instead? How did they feel about this? How did they put things right?

- Talk about the importance of saying 'sorry' to the people who have been upset by their actions. Remind them that this can also make the person feel better.

- Place children into groups of three or four. Invite them to make up a short play about someone doing something wrong, blaming others and the consequences that follow. Remind the children that each little play should demonstrate how the perpetrator put things right.

- Invite the groups in turn to show their plays to the others. Encourage the others to comment on them and to rate the effectiveness of how things were put right.

Franklin Watts
This edition published in Great Britain in 2016 by The Watts Publishing Group

Copyright text © The Watts Publishing Group 2014
Copyright illustrations © Trevor Dunton 2014

The right of Trevor Dunton to be identified as the illustrator
of this Work has been asserted in accordance with the
Copyright, Designs and Patents Act, 1988.

Series Editor: Jackie Hamley
Series Designer: Cathryn Gilbert

A CIP catalogue record for this book is available
from the British Library.

ISBN 978 1 4451 4720 8 (pbk)
ISBN 978 1 4451 2772 9 (library ebook)

Printed in China

Franklin Watts
An imprint of
Hachette Children's Group
Part of The Watts Publishing Group
Carmelite House
50 Victoria Embankment
London EC4Y 0DZ

An Hachette UK Company
www.hachette.co.uk

www.franklinwatts.co.uk

FSC
www.fsc.org
MIX
Paper from
responsible sources
FSC® C104740